# Wild Rapids

Alison Hawes • Jon Stuart

D1440215

## Contents

**OXFORD**
UNIVERSITY PRESS

**Macro Marvel**
(billionaire inventor)

# Welcome to Micro World!

*Macro Marvel* invented Micro World – a micro-sized theme park where you have to shrink to get in.

A computer called **CODE** controls Micro World and all the robots inside – MITEs and BITEs.

A MITE

A BITE

# Disaster strikes!

CODE goes wrong on opening day.
CODE wants to shrink the world.

Macro Marvel is trapped inside the park …

# Enter Team X!

Four micro agents – **Max**, **Cat**, **Ant** and **Tiger** – are sent to rescue Macro Marvel and defeat CODE.

**Mini Marvel** joins Team X.

**Mini Marvel**
(Macro's daughter)

# In the last book ...

* Max and Ant found the Spider-BITE.

* The Spider-BITE chased them. It fired its web but got trapped in the sticky plants.

* Max and Ant got the CODE key.

**CODE key
(4 collected)**

You are in the Jungle Trail zone.

3

# Before you read

## Sound checker
Say the sound.

### ea

## Sound spotter
Blend the sounds.

| d | ee | p |
|---|----|---|

| c | r | ea | k |
|---|---|----|---|

| s | t | ea | m | y |
|---|---|----|---|---|

| s | c | r | ea | m | ed |
|---|---|---|----|---|----|

## Tricky words
many
oh
any

## Into the zone
Can Team X and Mini avoid the
dangers and find the exit?

# Keep Off!

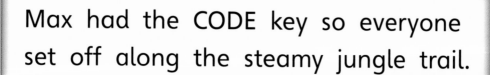

Max had the CODE key so everyone set off along the steamy jungle trail.

Soon they reached a deep canyon with a ropeway.

Keep off

"Cool!" said Tiger, as he and Ant started to run across it.

"Tiger! Ant! Stop!" shouted Mini. "It says 'Keep off'! The MITEs are repairing the ropeway!"

The ropes started to creak. Many of them completely snapped! "Oh no! Hurry!" screamed Mini. Tiger and Ant just made it across.

"Is there any way we can reach the exit?" cried Max.

Mini looked on her Gizmo.

"Only if we go down these rapids," she gulped.

# Now you have read ...
# Keep Off!

## Take a closer look

How did Mini know the ropeway
was dangerous? Look back
through the story. What did
Ant and Tiger miss?

## Thinking time

The team are stuck on either side of
the canyon. What are they thinking?

# Before you read

### Sound checker
Say the sound.

## ea

## Sound spotter
Blend the sounds.

| r | ea | ch |
| --- | --- | --- |

| l | ea | n | ed |
| --- | --- | --- | --- |

| c | l | ear | l | y |
| --- | --- | --- | --- | --- |

| r | ee | d | s |
| --- | --- | --- | --- |

### Tricky words
any
many
oh

## Into the zone
What do you think will happen
to Max, Cat, Mini and Rex on
the rapids?

12

# A Risky River Trip

Max, Cat and Mini went down to the river. They needed a boat to take them to the exit.

"I can't see any boats," said Max.
Then Mini spied some rafts hidden
in the reeds.
"Let's use one of these," she said.

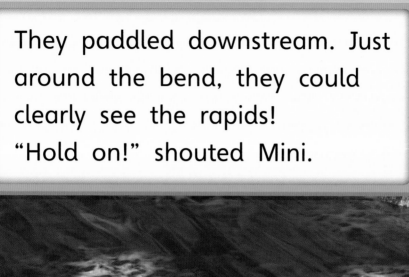

They paddled downstream. Just around the bend, they could clearly see the rapids!
"Hold on!" shouted Mini.

The raft spun round many times. Cat was tossed into the river.

"Oh no! Help!" she screamed.

Max leaned out to help Cat but he couldn't reach her.
"Can anyone help us? Get the Green Dart!" yelled Max.

Ant and Tiger scrambled down to the river. Tiger reached for Max's backpack.

Tiger took out the Green Dart and they made it bigger.

They rescued Cat first.

Then they rushed off to help the others.

Team X, Mini and Rex set off for the exit at top speed.

"I hope that will be the last extreme adventure for me!" said Cat.
She put in the CODE key to open the door.

Now you have read ...
# A Risky River Trip

To get to the next zone we have to read the CODE words. Then the exit door will open. Can you help us read them?

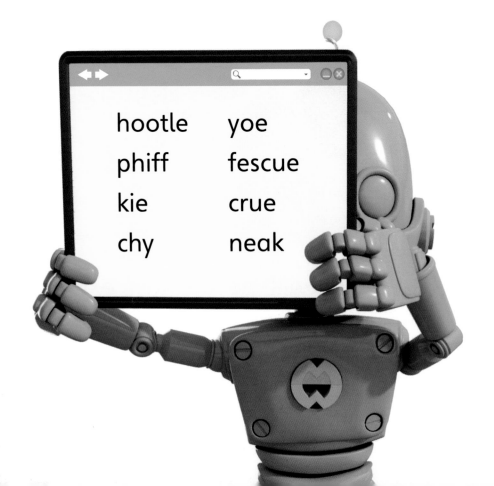

hootle     yoe

phiff      fescue

kie        crue

chy        neak